Rufferella

For Mum, with thanks for all her efforts to turn us into real girls ...

Text copyright © 2000 Vanessa Gill Brown
Illustrations copyright © 2000 Mandy Stanley

All rights reserved. Published by Scholastic Inc.,
Publishers since 1920, by arrangement with Bloomsbury Publishing Plc.
SCHOLASTIC and associated logos are trademarks and/or registered trademarks of Scholastic Inc.

Library of Congress Cataloging-in-publication Data Available
ISBN 0 439 26165 1

10 9 8 7 6 5 4 3 2 1   01 01 03 04
Printed in Hong Kong and China
First American paperback, September 2001

Rufferella

Vanessa Gill-Brown and Mandy Stanley

    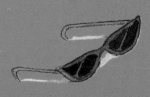

Diamante loved stories and her most favorite was
Cinderella. She liked to imagine that she was the
fairy godmother – the one who made things happen.
She desperately wanted to turn something into
something – but what?

One day, her eyes rested on Ruff, her dog. Aha! She would turn her dog into … into … a human, into a Ruff-erella!

"How about it Ruff?" she exclaimed. "Want to be a girl?"

Ruff didn't really like being a human much. But Diamante could be very convincing, and soon, Ruff was sure it was all trifle and television in the human world. But how would it happen?

She didn't even have a magic wand.

"I don't need one," said Diamante confidently. "I will teach you how to be human. It isn't difficult. I do it all the time without even thinking."

So the lessons began.
First Diamante dressed
Ruff in human clothes,

did her hair in a human
style, and applied some
makeup.

"There!" she squealed. "At least you look like a real
girl now! And you shall be called Rufferella."

Next Rufferella learned how to eat with a knife and fork, drink from a cup, and how to cough and sneeze politely.

Diamante also tried to explain about not taking all the chocolate cookies for yourself, but Rufferella found this aspect of being human very difficult to swallow (unlike the chocolate cookies).

Look at it her way – finally allowed to eat human treats and she's supposed to let others choose first? Sausages in particular would have posed a problem – Rufferella loved those more than anything.

Ahem.
Atishoo!

Diamante decided to show her off at a friend's birthday party.
"You shall go to the ball, Rufferella! Well, Penny's party
anyway. But you mustn't let anyone know you're really a
dog."

Rufferella was nervous, but she had no need to be. She danced, played games, drank soda, ate cake, and all without spilling a drop or a crumb. She even sang happy birthday to Penny.

To everyone's delight she had the most beautiful, deep voice anyone at the party had ever heard.

"What a wonderful voice this girl has – she should be on television!"

After that, she was invited to sing at other people's parties, then in theatres, where crowds came to hear the amazingly sweet, low voice of little Rufferella. And eventually she did sing on TV.

Diamante always went with her, but she couldn't help feeling a bit left out. There was no time for playing soccer or rolling around on the carpet, like they used to. Still, it was fun being Rufferella's assistant.

One day, among the usual heap of mail for Rufferella, a very special invitation came. Diamante opened it.

"It's from the Queen! She saw you on television and wants you – and a guest – to attend a ball at the palace! You really are Rufferella!"

"Splendid," said Rufferella.

So Diamante replied to the Queen, accepting her kind invitation and they both set about getting new dresses and hairdo's.

The ball was wonderful. Everything was bright and sparkling and beautiful. Everyone wanted to dance with Rufferella and compliment her on her charming — and unusual — singing voice.

Then they were escorted to the dining room.

Rufferella was worried – Diamante's place was miles away.
She'd never been totally on her own before and she was
hungry. And the prince next to her was just a tiny bit
stupid and boring and the dress was just a little bit tight …
      She wondered what was for dinner. She watched as the
Queen was served. It was sausages. SAUSAGES!!
Rufferella took one look and leapt on to the table,
bounding toward the Queen.

Rufferella landed on the Queen's plate and
began wolfing the delicious, juicy sausages.
　"Good heavens, she's a DOG! Rufferella is a dog! No
wonder she had such an unusual singing voice. Catch her!"
exclaimed the people. Then Rufferella took another flying
leap, this time landing in Diamante's arms. Together, they
ran out of the palace and all the way home.

Next morning, there was less mail than usual, but there was a package for Rufferella. She was feeling miserable and didn't want to look at it. So Diamante opened it and took out something hard, wrapped in tissue. There was a note with it which read:

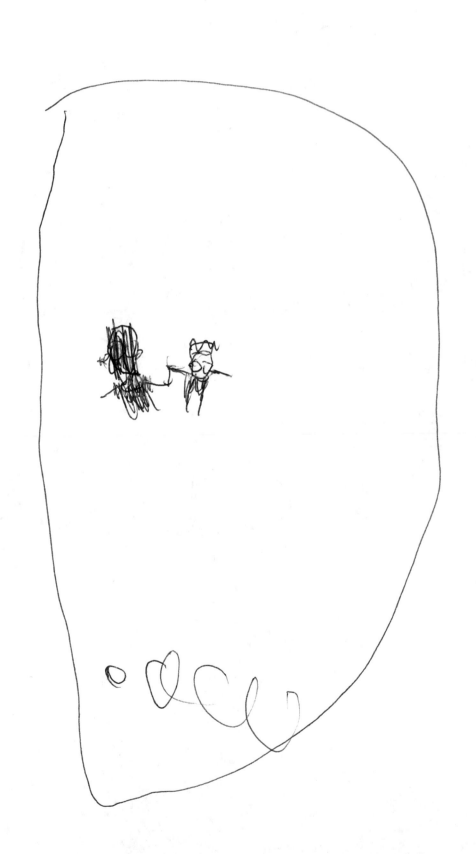

Dinomite worked so hard on making Ruffurella real, that ~~onzone~~ after the insudent at the Cassle Ruff became real and was known as Ruffurella,

And They Lived Happley Ever After...

The end

(she maride the prince.)

Dear 'Rufferella'

Please do not worry about the unfortunate events at the ball (sausages are hard to resist after all). A little piece of royal advice: One is often best off if one allows one to be oneself. By this I mean that while I make a reasonable job of being Queen, I should make a pig's ear of being a popstar.

Take care dear,
Queen

Diamante unwrapped the item.

"It's a dog's bowl!" she cried. Rufferella was so pleased that a tear came to her eye.

"Can I use it?" she asked. "If it's all the same to you, I think I'll give up being a human, and my singing career. It's just not me."

"Oh, good," replied Diamante, "I've really missed having you as my pet."

Ruff smiled and said, "No more Rufferella?"

"No more Rufferella," agreed Diamante.

"How about a trip to the park to play catch?" asked Diamante. Ruff yelped in agreement and off they went.
Everything was back to normal.